I0760716

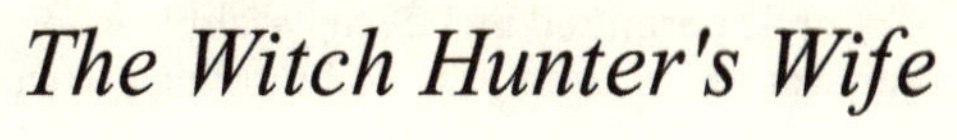

*The Witch Hunter's Wife*

Content Guidance: This book contains several scenes depicting pregnancy loss, PTSD, suicidal ideation, and an on page hanging. The infant deaths are not described in detail.

Published by Shoreshouse

PO Box 51

Ogden, KS 66517

United States

To access the Shoreshouse Private Library or subscribe to the Shoreshouse Journal, visit the author's website at www.jessicalunt.com

ISBN: 978-1-969195-00-6 (hardcover)

*a short story*

# THE WITCH HUNTER'S WIFE

JESSICA LUNT

SHORESHOUSE

BOOKS BY JESSICA LUNT

*The Witch Hunter's Wife*
*A Bouquet of Blue Sailors* (Feb 2026)

*For the ones born sleeping,*
*For the ones we carried but never held,*
*For those we held but could not take home,*
*For those who came home but could not stay,*
*And for the arms that ache to hold them still.*

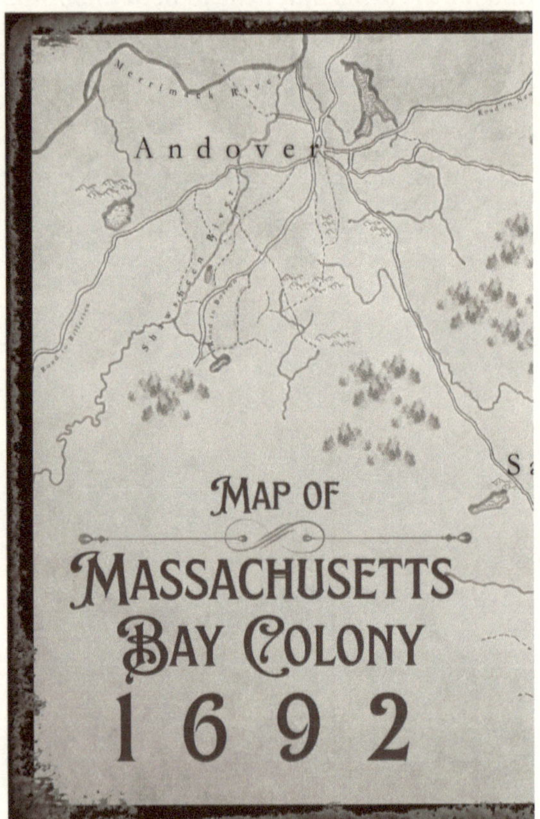
Merrimack River
Andover
Shawsheen River
MAP OF
MASSACHUSETTS
BAY COLONY
1692

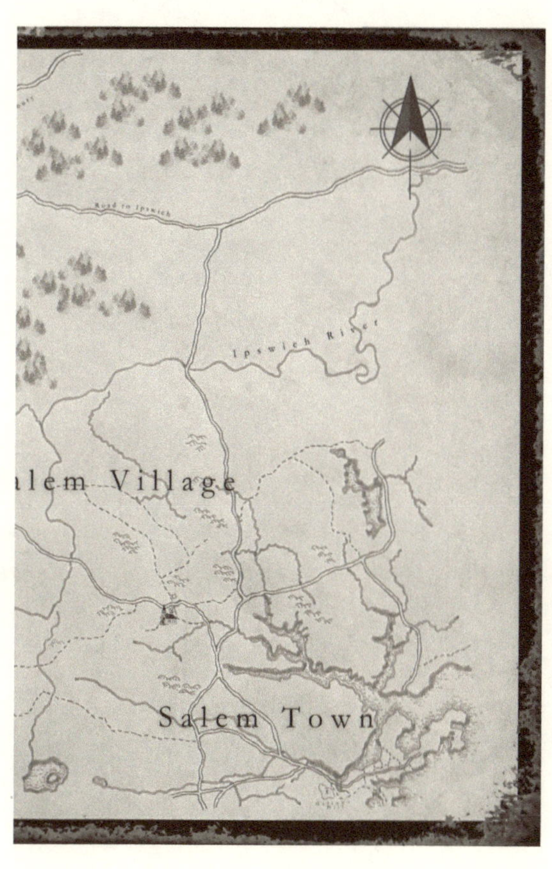
Road to Ipswich
Ipswich River
alem Village
Salem Town

1

# THE VILLAGE, APRIL 19TH, 1692

"Bridget Bishop," Judge Hathorne said from his seat upon the dais. "You are brought before this body of authority to give an account of your familiarity of, and with the acts of witchcraft."

The older woman looked about the crowded room of Salem Village's meetinghouse, fight evident in the set of her jaw. She stood before the pulpit, her deep red skirts within reach of the first few rows.

Caroline Choate averted her eyes. She didn't wish to be here, to see their Salem Town neighbor, the outspoken Bridget Bishop, dragged before her peers and charged with accusations so severe. But John had wished to come.

"You all are a witness that I am clear of any such acts!" The wool ends of Bridget's coat snapped as she turned to face the young girls, her accusers. They responded with tortured moans, twisting their bodies upon the pew.

John's hand came atop of Caroline's before her fingers could begin their wringing. She was glad of the comfort. The growing crowds for these examinations had made the esquires order men and women to sit together instead of sitting separate as they did in church. Like many in the area, John had taken a deep interest in Salem's recent unrest, wishing to discuss witchcraft at home far past Caroline's comfort, even to the point of suggesting its existence as a cause for her infirmities. Today's outing was a natural extension of his curiosity and desires for her welfare.

"Hath this woman hurt you?" Murmured assents from the young girls followed Hathorne's question. "You are hereby accused of hurting these five young girls, Bridget Bishop. What do you have to say?"

John's hand gently squeezed Caroline's as Bridget's words slipped through gritted teeth. "I have never seen them before. Neither have I ever set foot in this village before today!"

Several accusations came out at once from the girls. Their words echoed through the growing heat of the room.

"She tempted me to sign the book of the devil!"

"She caused great pains to come upon me!"

"My brother tore her coat while fighting off her dark spectral!"

Hathorne bit into this last declaration like a starved dog. "Let us examine the coat."

Caroline craned her neck around knitted caps and white bonnets. Surely such a claim would be easily refuted and they could all go home. But a rip was found in Bridget's black coat and whispers of *"witch"* passed through the room.

John's reassuring gaze peeked between the dark hairs of his full beard. Another gentle squeeze of the hands. Another unspoken request to stay. He wanted to see how it would end, but Caroline feared she already knew. It would end as all the others had ended.

Hathorne cleared his throat. "Bridget Bishop. It is said you bewitched your first husband to his death."

"I am no witch. It was already declared so ten years ago, in Salem Town." Bridget rolled her eyes and the accusing girls followed in kind, their eyes rolling into the back of their heads as they fainted upon the floor. "You cannot think to try me again when I am innocent."

"Are you not worried for the pains these girls have endured? What do you think of them being such afflicted?"

Bridget huffed a disbelieving breath. "I do not know what to think of them."

Caroline was familiar with this side of Bridget, and in other circumstances she might have laughed. But now was not the time for the older woman's obstinate humor. Did Bridget not understand? She had to know what had happened to the others.

"Are you not familiar with the Devil?" Hathorne continued.

"I am not familiar with the Devil. I tell you

again, I am innocent." Bridget shook her head. "I do not even know what a witch is."

Hathorne raised an eyebrow. "If you do not know what a witch is, how do you know you are not one?"

Bridget's defiant stare sent a chill down Caroline's spine. "Let me be clear, Mr. Hathorne. If I was one, you would know."

Murmurs spilled over from the galley seats above them. Caroline tried to shrink back, but the weight of John's hands anchored her feet to the floor. The bodies in the row behind her were too close. The smell of smoke-filled coats pressed in around her. There was no place to go.

Hathorne's voice deepened, displaying his authority. "You may threaten, but you will not be permitted to act out in harm."

"I tell you I am innocent!"

Hathorne continued over Bridget's words. "There have been others who confessed earlier today. They claim themselves and your person all to be witches."

"I have heard nothing of this."

"That is a lie, Bridget Bishop!" The slap of his hand against hard wood silenced everyone in the room. "We have told you ourselves such information preceding this examination!"

The older woman fixed her stare into the dark

wood of the pulpit behind Hathorne. "I am innocent. I know nothing of anyone being accused of such acts either."

Hathorne ignored her final plea. "Bridget Bishop. Upon hearing and seeing with our own eyes the stated evidence, we commit thee with charges of witchcraft."

A burning sensation filled Caroline's throat. Ten people of Salem Town and Village had been arrested, examined, and charged with witchcraft in less than two months. People she had thought to be ordinary, if somewhat flawed individuals, much like herself. Witchcraft was a capital crime, one that condemned the soul. Could it truly be that Bridget also had involved herself with such devilish matters? Sickness threatened to escape her mouth at the thought. She turned to John to plead her excuse.

"Wait for me outside," he whispered into her ear.

Caroline didn't need any encouragement to escape. She stood outside at the entrance of the meetinghouse with little relief, nodding salutations to all who passed her by. Most took no notice of her, too caught up in recounting that morning's examination of Bridget Bishop to each other. Their whispers made her clutch the linen kerchief covering her chest a little tighter.

Spring in the Massachusetts Bay Colony was a fickle mistress. Some days it promised the long languid heat of summer. Other days, the tickling cold of winter. Today it held neither of those comforts as Caroline breathed in the sand and pine and pain of her new reality. There were witches in Salem.

At last, John took his turn exiting the meetinghouse doors. His face betrayed none of his thoughts. But after ten years of marriage, she could guess his mood. He was not happy.

Caroline took his offered arm as they walked to their horse and cart. "What will happen to Bridget now?" She kept her voice low, though there were few around them anymore to overhear her.

John glanced at the others walking home in the distance. "There is no court created for such cases. There has not been one for some time. They will hold her at the jail in Salem Town with the others until she can be tried. And if she is found guilty, her property will fall to the court." His tone matched her own, low and careful to show little emotion. "She may not have cursed you, but I had hoped that as her nearest neighbor we would be consulted in her charges."

Caroline ignored his comment about her latent nightmares, wishing to return to the details of Bridget's case instead. "What of her husband,

Edward? They would take away his land when it is his wife who is charged, not him?"

John shook his head as he handed her up into the cart. "Bridget brought her own property into the marriage. An inheritance from her late husband that included a house, ten acres, and two pigs." His voice caught in a grunt as he heaved himself into the cart. "Edward has no right to it. Unless she has named him in her will, it will all go to the children born by her through her first and second husbands."

She stared in thought as John arranged himself in the seat beside her. Bridget had mentioned a feud between herself and her stepchildren over her late husband's will. Caroline hadn't realized Bridget had inherited such a large amount.

John snapped the reins and their gelding pulled the cart forward onto the street. "But they will get none of it if she is convicted. No family will get their inheritance if any of the arrested are convicted."

"Are there a great deal of women in Salem who own property?"

John huffed. "Too many if you ask me. And not just in Salem. All over the Massachusetts Bay Colony. For a society where it is men who make the laws and serve the justice, it is an oddity that so many women should hold power with their property."

The wheels of the cart rolled over the dirt road and the rough wood of the seat chafed against her backside. She preferred walking to the stiffness of riding in the cart. John rode the gelding whenever he traveled alone. But he had long insisted they travel this way when together.

The silence stretched and the trees thickened too soon around them. "We are headed north?"

"Yes."

"I've not had the chance to stock the larder since last summer."

John kissed the side of her head. "Thomas and Martha will have us. I have business with Thomas I've put off for far too long."

Caroline nodded, taking comfort in his gesture. It was a relief not to return to their house in Salem Town. The past ten years had given her and John time to cultivate their differences within their marriage. He with his desire for the industry in Salem, and she with her preference for the neighboring town of Andover. She thought of their Salem house again and shuddered. She would never love Salem the way John did.

# THE TOWN, SEPTEMBER 1682, TEN YEARS PRIOR

*"Oh John, what have you done?" Caroline looked upon the house before them, with its dark trim roof and broken white-washed walls. It was small when compared to the others upon the street, and it warned of neglect. But it was a building budding with quaint importance in a promising town.*

*John took her hands in his, his excitement barely contained. "I have secured us a house, my dear. One we can build our future in."*

*If they were somewhere more private she knew with clarity the type of kiss he would have given her in that moment. Hard. Hungry. Helpless in his love for her. But such things were not to be enjoyed in public. And certainly not out upon the streets of Salem Town. The imaginings of it almost cured her of her dismay.*

*"But the expense! John, we have land in Andover. I thought you wished to build there. I heard you speaking with Goodman Allen about making improvements upon it in the spring." They had set out on their own, away from family, only a few months ago. Andover had been the perfect beginning, with land ripe for plantings and a community filled with children and families to care for them.*

*"I will keep my agreements with Goodman Allen.*

*But there is opportunity here now, Caroline. Goodman Beadle has said so. Salem Town is where those with true influence reside. Where we can raise our station in life." John moved their hands to cradle her swollen belly, his face growing older with concern. "And we must get a proper roof over your head before winter. I cannot raise a barn so fast, nor would I have our child born in such a lowly state."*

*Caroline smoothed away the worry from his brow, unable to resist touching him. "You forget, John, that the greatest of all men was born in a stable. And if it was enough for he, then it is enough for me."*

*He caught her hand and placed a tender kiss upon her palm. The intensity of his gaze caught her breath.*

*"I do not need a grand house to live in," she whispered, losing herself in his unspoken devotions. "I only need you."*

*"I am yours, my dearest Caroline." His words were hot against her palm, his stubble rough against her smooth skin. "Let me show you. Let me give you this." His nearness muddled her thoughts and when she did not reply, John smiled. "Would you like to see inside it?"*

*Caroline nodded, still unable to speak.*

*The air was cooler inside with a dampness that spoke of unuse. Soot and bits of charred wood coated the hearth of each fireplace. There were four rooms total: a kitchen and three others to be used for living and sleeping. John led her through them all, painting visions for her. Little feet tapping against a supper table as they read from the family Bible. Home-sewn quilts draped over children's beds built from the lumber of the trees right outside. It was beautiful. Every inch of it was beautiful.*

*Caroline tugged upon his hands as they stood in the final room, the one that was meant for their unborn child. "But what of the expense, John?"*

*"Never mind the expense, Caroline. I have made an arrangement with Goodman Beadle."*

*"How can I not worry when it is the future of our family we speak of?"*

*John's smile was warm with adoration as his hands traveled up the back of her arms, comforting her fears with his soothing touch. "Goodman Beadle wishes to open an inn or two within Salem Town. But the man is injured from King Philip's War and cannot do it alone. I have offered to be his partner. He has agreed to lease us this home and its orchard in exchange for the first five years of my part of our earnings."*

*"And the land in Andover?"*

*He kissed her then, his soft lips pressing into hers with amusement. "You took an exceptional liking to that town." He kissed her again this time with tender promise. "Do not worry, my dear. I have not forgotten Andover. We will use the land there to grow wheat or corn each year, whichever Goodman Allen determines will yield the most profit." His mouth hovered over hers.*

*"And then?" she whispered against his lips.*

*"And then, Goody Choate," he whispered as his hand fumbled with the hooks of her waistcoat, "I suspect we will be brimming with so many little ones, I will have to build us a bigger house."*

## ANDOVER, APRIL 19TH, 1692

Martha Carrier stayed Caroline's hands. "Do not trouble yourself. Sarah will take care of it."

"But you fed us on such short notice. It is no small feat to cook for your family of seven, plus John and I."

Martha waved Caroline's protest away and her daughter, Sarah, took the plate from her hands. The youngest, Hannah, slipped from Caroline's lap, leaving behind her doll as she toddled dutifully after Sarah, unable to carry more than a couple napkins at only three years old.

"I used to cook for nine." Martha's wrinkled eyes lingered on Sarah's and Hannah's faces. "It is no trouble, Caroline, really. You and John are always welcome here. We've not enjoyed such company very often of late. Not since the smallpox came through."

Caroline's heart went out to the older woman. She knew what it was like to lose a child, even if it was not in the way Martha had endured. Easily twenty years Caroline's senior, Martha had been the one to help pull her out of her grief. She had not had anyone but John that first time, ten years ago, when they were so new to Salem Town. He'd been devastated but still caring of her then and through the other losses that followed. But it was

Martha who had helped Caroline accept her fate: that each stirring in her womb would grow still. That she would bleed and then she would lose one child and then another.

Caroline squeezed Martha's hand. She opened her mouth to console and to thank Martha again, for it was a great blessing to be so far removed from the accusations in Salem, but she was interrupted by the voices of the men.

"I've told ye before, John, that land's Martha's. I'll not be having a say in what happens to it."

"Andrew Allen made to offer it to me, Thomas. We spoke of it that summer, a few months before he died. And he was of sound mind. You know he was."

"Aye, I can attest to that. Right to the very end. But facts is, that land's hers. Speak to Martha if ye still want it that bad."

"What's this?" Martha sat up straight, pulling her hands away from Caroline's grip.

John took a deep breath. "Your father and I made a deal. The west meadows and your access to the Shawsheen River would be given to me upon my payment of thirty pounds in wheat."

"You've said this before, John. But I've not seen any record that those were his wishes other than your word, and your word alone. It's not a fair trade."

"You seemed to think it was valuable enough when I brought the grain to you two winters ago. When nothing else was left to fill your stores after the smallpox robbed you of harvesting a crop."

"That was in payment for the cows he sold to Caroline in the spring," Martha said. "Which was at your request, mind you. He never would have demanded so little if he meant for it to cover the meadows to feed the cows as well."

"But the land, Martha. I need the land. And your father – well, you have no use for it. Or the access to the river."

"Oh, not you too, John. I've heard it enough from Benjamin Abbot. Don't tell me you're on his side."

John grounded his teeth as his words dripped with accusation. "The man has a point, Martha. You would do well to see it."

"Those borders were decided long before you and Caroline ever thought of coming here. It's my father's land and I'll not part with it because some man decides he wants it. I expected better from you, John. But perhaps you too should be cursed for your covetous desires."

John slumped back in his chair, but his eyes narrowed in Martha's direction. He didn't take kindly to having his character questioned so.

Caroline reached for John's hand. His aggression had grown in the past few years, but it was nothing her touch couldn't soothe. "I'm sure there's something we can work out. Goodman Allen wouldn't have wanted to leave us without a way to care for those cows. Right, Martha?"

The front door slammed, ending the conversation. Heavy footsteps made their way to the kitchen. The Carrier's three sons, Richard, Andrew, and Thomas Jr., stopped at the entrance. The younger two were dirty and their clothing looked ill-worn even for their wiry forms. Richard's cheek, however, was a mottled red and blue, forewarning a bruise.

Thomas stood, instantly filling the space with his bristling gray hair and hulking frame. He took in the state of his sons. The three of them fidgeted under his disapproval.

At eighteen, only Richard came close to matching his father in stature. He wiped at the split in his lip and cleared his throat. "Da. Ma. Goodman Choate. Goody Choate." He nodded to each, then ushered his younger brothers forward.

"Is that all ye have to say for yourselves?"

The boys ignored their father and sat at the table. Thomas Jr. reached for the bread loaf but Martha stopped him, scolding him with her eyes.

Thomas spoke again. "What happened?"

Thomas Jr. glanced at his father, and then his brothers. But Richard and Andrew refused to speak. “There was a fight.”

“Aye, I can see that,” Thomas said. “And who was it that was worth sullying your clothes for?”

“No one,” Richard said. His words silenced anything else his brothers might have said. “Andrew and Thomas didn’t fight.”

“Richard,” Martha said, love and exasperation infused in her tone.

“I stepped in. It wasn’t their fault, Ma. And the smallpox wasn’t our fault either.”

Caroline looked between them with concern. “Surely you aren’t still being blamed? There were many others who could have brought it into Andover.”

“You know how people are, Caroline,” Martha said. “Once they get an idea planted in their head, it’s rather hard to root it out. We’ve not been allowed in church for two years. My uncle has spoken for us, but even his standing as a reverend has not shielded us.” She turned back to Richard. “Was it the usual again?”

“Allen was there too.”

“Your cousin?” Thomas asked.

Richard nodded and Thomas huffed. Martha pulled her husband down into his seat.

“We ought to get your sister to take him back to Billerica.”

“He’s twenty-two years old, Thomas. Roger and

Mary cannot force him to stay with them."

"Let him use those spells he's been about."

"He doesn't use spells. Roger is no more a witch than I am, Thomas. You should not speak such things. You know what is happening in Salem."

John cleared his throat. He laced his fingers with Caroline's, now held beneath the table, pulling her attention back to his side. "We should get going. We'll leave your family to its business."

Thomas stood. "I'll walk ye out."

John retrieved the lap blanket for Caroline as she arranged herself in the seat of the cart. They didn't have far to go, but the spring nights still clung to their memories of winter.

"I'm sorry ye didn't get the news ye wanted, John." Thomas rubbed the back of his neck.

John refused to meet the older man's gaze as he climbed into the cart. His silence as he grabbed the reins spoke of his hurt loud enough. He moved to usher the gelding forward but suspended his hands in the air. "Maybe if you were more of a man in your own house, Thomas, your family would not be in the state it is now."

Caroline sucked in a breath at the insult, but she didn't attempt to reprove John. It would only injure his pride more.

Thomas didn't flinch. "I've learned not to interfere with Martha's affairs. She knows what she's doing. But my sons are still a bit wet behind the ears. They'll learn in time which fights they can and cannot win."

"I hope they learn soon then. For their own sakes." John snapped the reins, not waiting for Thomas's reply.

The old Allen homestead, where Martha and Thomas resided, dipped out of view as their cart ambled along the dirt-packed road.

"John," Caroline said after they had traveled for several moments in silence.

He took a deep breath beside her. His disappointments were often hard for them to wade through and she reached her arm across his back. His heavy hand settled upon her thigh and he squeezed. He would need time to get over this slight.

The twelve-room saltbox house appeared behind the familiar bend of trees, its stature intimidating even in the darkness of night. But only to those who weren't familiar with it. John took Caroline's hand, careful to guide her through their home's wide doors. A single candlestick lit their path up the stairs as John lifted it in front of them. It cast comforting shadows on their thoughts in the silence. Tonight would bring peaceful sleep — away from the unrest in Salem.

John removed his doublet and breeches before

returning to Caroline. The loose sleeves of his shirt exposed the dark hair of his forearms as he helped her remove her waistcoat and petticoats. He kissed her gently between the removal of each piece of clothing. Their movements were practiced though, without excitement or longing.

Her body felt heavy without the support of her outer garments. Her curves had filled out over the years, their softness increasing greatly this past winter. John left her to stand exposed in her linen smock while he fetched the thick blanket for the bed, but there were no invitations to explore each other more. There had not been for some time. They laid together in the dark, John's warmth wrapped around Caroline as the chill edged through the empty echoes of the house. Tomorrow would be a new day. She prayed the horrors that had ravaged Salem these past two months would be put to rest with its light.

# 2

## THE TOWN, NOVEMBER 1684, EIGHT YEARS PRIOR

*Caroline's breath caught. All was silent in the house. The snow outside had blanketed many of nature's sounds. John was out in Andover and wouldn't be back for hours. No one else was there to help confirm her suspicions. She placed a shaking hand upon her middle.*

Thump.

*The quickening movement brought an unexplained terror to her heart.*

Thump. Thump.

*The child was strong, shouldering a small portion of her fears. But it was not enough to fight the sense of foreboding threatening to rob her of her celebration. Tears puddled in the corners of her eyes as she fought for her hope. She had suspected the pregnancy these last two months but had convinced herself it was not so. Not after the devastating death of their firstborn two years ago. Josiah Choate had never taken a breath.*

*Footsteps outside strained Caroline's senses again. The footsteps were heavy and fast approaching. Caroline braced herself as the front door opened and a man entered their home.*

*"John?" She took a tentative step toward him.*

*Her mind told her it was him, but his movements were clumsy and unfamiliar to her.*

*"Caroline!" John's voice was too loud and his breath too sweet. He enveloped her within his arms, eliciting a small squeak from her mouth. He chuckled.*

*"You're back early."*

*John's sigh was deep against her. "Goodman Allen met me in town. Bought me a few drinks after hearing what the others are saying. Official news came in from England. The Massachusetts Bay Colony charter has been revoked."*

*Caroline tipped her head back to meet his gaze. "Revoked? But what does this mean?"*

*John shrugged and her body moved with his. "We are without law. Only religion is left to govern us with ministers we pay from our own pockets. Our land in Andover may not be ours. This house we have spent two years leasing may not be Goodman Beadle's to give us. No one in the colony knows if they have rights to what they own anymore."*

*Caroline shifted her worries to John and squeezed him within his embrace. She understood better now. Alcohol was not forbidden, when not in excess. But he only turned to the drink when fear overwhelmed him. Her heart went out to him. "Perhaps I can bring you some words of comfort."*

*John studied her face, tracing his finger along*

*her cheek before tucking a piece of hair behind her ear. "And what words of comfort would you have for me?"*

*She swallowed and willed herself to speak with a brightness she did not feel. "I am with child."*

*His eyes widened, but he did not speak. Caroline brought his hands down and placed them upon her belly, bolstering herself through his touch.*

*"A moment of patience, John," she whispered, "and then we will feel the life that is inside me."*

*He waited with her, and his devoted stillness brought a smile to her face. It was this devotion that had first won her over. Devotion to her comfort. Her words. Her body. Her dreams.*

Thump.

*John's eyes met hers with wonder. A tear slipped down between the beginnings of his dark whiskers. Then he took her face in his hands. Hands that made her wish to sigh.*

*"Thank you." He kissed her lips. "Thank you, my dearest Caroline. If only I had a gift for you."*

# ANDOVER, APRIL 20TH, 1692

Caroline woke to the heated press of John's lips upon her own and familiar flutters stirred within her belly. She often dreamed of her past pregnancies, feeling the specters of her children moving inside her – even after waking. When she had first told John of them he had looked at her with such horror, she thought he would call for the doctor. She had since learned from Martha and the other women in Andover that these spectral stirrings were normal. But they always left her with a deep longing to visit her children's graves. John wouldn't wish to, but she could.

She blinked twice, wiping away the remnants of sleep as her vision focused. John's hearty smile hovered above her and she sighed with relief at the sight. His mood had passed.

"Good morning, my dearest," he said, his voice gravely.

Caroline stretched beneath him. "Good morning." The room was bright around them. Too bright. John must have pulled back the curtains.

"You slept most of the morning away. Very unlike you." The back of his hand pressed against her forehead. He frowned.

"What is it?"

"I was to leave on business today." He pressed

her cheeks. “You are not feverish.”

“I feel well enough. What business?”

“In Amesbury. I will be back before the end of the week.”

“When are you to leave?” Caroline’s head swam with the news as she sat up. John seldom had business beyond Andover. She could not think what would draw him away to a town as far as Amesbury, which lay nearly twenty miles to the north of Andover.

John moved off of her. “I will ride out after today’s services.” He studied her as she clutched her head from the dizziness. “Are you sure you are not unwell? Your color has turned.”

“I think I sat up too swiftly. I will be fine.”

“You are sure?”

She reached for his hand. “I will be fine,” she repeated with a squeeze. “I can seek out Martha for a tincture if it would ease your worries.”

“No. I would prefer that you stay away from Martha Carrier while I am gone. Remain at the house in Salem Town where you are closer to others. Call upon the Higginsons if you have need.”

She puzzled at his words of warning and his mood. John knew it was difficult enough for Caroline to stay in Salem when he was there. With him, her memories could be dissuaded, and their horrors need not be relived. But without him, things were sure to grow worse. "If you are to leave after the services, how am I to return there with the cart? You will need the horse, yes?"

John bit his lip but he did not answer her. Instead, he pulled her to stand, then rushed to retrieve her clothes. Caroline reached up in duty to help him with his clothing, but he pressed her petticoats into her hands. He had already dressed.

"We shall figure it out at the meetinghouse, before the end of services," he said, helping Caroline tie her petticoats and fasten her waistcoat. "Your indulgence this morning has left us little time to discuss it now if we do not wish to be late."

Guilt encompassed Caroline's heart, swallowing the small hurt from John's uncharacteristically careless plan for her return to Salem. She had not meant to exhibit such laziness. But yesterday had been a long day between Bridget's examination, the travel out to Andover, and their late supper with the Carriers.

John tugged on the ties of her bonnet, pulling her attention back to his face. "I could not bear it if something were to happen to you. Please seek out our neighbors should any needs arise. Do not isolate yourself, like you are prone to do."

Caroline's heart hummed at the sincerity within his eyes. Past experience had told her his statement to be true. He had not overlooked the manner of her return to Salem Town because he did not care for her. No, there was some other cause for his inaction.

She wandered about the rooms, stretching her limbs still heavy from sleep and shaking away her nervous thoughts of returning to Salem, as John prepared the horse and cart. Even with the home's lingering emptiness, Caroline preferred to stay out here in Andover than return to their house in Salem Town where their neighbors were being accused of witchcraft.

John had built this saltbox house, with two stories at the front and one in the back, after her second pregnancy. He hadn't waited until their lease with Goodman Beadle was fulfilled like promised, needing a project to give him hope after she had lost John Choate Jr., their second son. He thought it would give her hope. But it was never hope that she wrapped herself in when she walked through these rooms, with their empty pine-framed walls and blanket-covered beds. No, it was something more akin to resignation — a sense of nostalgia for her dreams and simpler griefs. And yet, it was preferable to the memories that threatened to wake each day under the summer beams at their home in Salem.

Two cups placed upon the table caught

Caroline's eye. Dregs of John's coffee lined the inside of one while the other wore a thin smell of beer. Someone had been here. A man, judging by the distance the chair had been pushed away from the table. The horse nickered outside and John's indulging voice answered it. Then his footsteps were at the door.

"Caroline?"

He caught her standing near the evidence of the morning. But it was his face that flashed with guilt, not hers. A brief moment that she would have missed if she had not been looking for it.

"The cart is ready, my dear."

They didn't keep secrets in their marriage. She could ask him. But she slipped her hand in the crook of his arm, holding in place the words she wished to say. Perhaps later.

Her backside ached from the seat in the cart as they drove. It would not improve while sitting upon the seats within the meetinghouse, and she fortified her expectations against any relief.

The younger of Andover's two ministers, Reverend Barnard, greeted them at the door. "It is good to see you again in our congregation this morning, Goodman Choate, Goody Choate."

"Likewise, Reverend Barnard," John answered for the both of them. "Will we be hearing from you or Reverend Dane today?"

Reverend Barnard gave John a wry smile. “He does not preach very much anymore, but Reverend Dane has prepared a special sermon.”

“Ah, then we have picked an opportune Sunday to attend here in Andover.”

“Yes. I have not been told much of what is planned. But I understand it is a sermon in response to Reverend Parris’s recent admonitions in Salem. It should prove to be quite… engaging.”

John lifted his eyebrow and Caroline tried not to smile. She did not begrudge listening to the sermons preached in Salem Town or Salem Village, but they had drifted far into fire and brimstone over the past month with all the witchcraft accusations. Martha Carrier’s aging uncle, Reverend Francis Dane, was an amiable man that tolerated no nonsense. He would bring a much-needed variety to Caroline’s and John’s worship. His age and outspoken nature might even prove his sermon to be more entertaining than enlightening.

“But please,” Reverend Barnard said, stepping to the side, “do not let me keep you. We will begin soon. I suggest you take your seats.”

John led Caroline to a bench on the women’s side. “I saw the Ballards as we walked in. I will try to speak to him about the arrangements needed to see you home.” He squeezed her hand, then moved to the men’s side.

The congregation hushed as Reverend Dane took his place at the pulpit. Caroline adjusted her posture on the backless bench and craned her neck above the others. She could not see the Ballards, and she had lost sight of John. Suspicion crept into her thoughts in the form of two cups as the sermon began with its usual praises of God and quoting of scripture.

"Ye have heard of what transpires across the river," Reverend Dane said. His timely words warred with Caroline's desire to discover where John had gone. "Ye have been told the Devil hath been raised amongst us. That our brothers and sisters in Salem are guilty of conspiring with him. Even of committing acts of witchcraft. I do not claim that witches do not exist. We all know they do. But I am here to tell ye that the Lord disavows the manner of those trials taking place across the river. It is not just. It is not godly. It is not what the Lord would have us do."

The collective breath of the congregation pulled Caroline's attention fully to the front. Reverend Dane's posture was stooped with age but his hand was raised, shaking with the fervor of his words.

"Spectral evidence is not sufficient to condemn any man, woman, or child, to live the life of the damned. We should not be in support of these trials. We should not even entertain their existence. I tell ye now, yea, the Devil very well may be among us. But that is because we let him. We let him scathe our thoughts. We let him bring us to act against our neighbor. We let his voice overpower our judgments. When shall the Devil be silenced? When we decide that he shall be so!" Reverend Dane's fists against the pulpit made more than one person flinch.

"The Bible teaches that only the Lord can know all our sins, our thoughts, and our desires," he continued. "Only the Lord knows which of us act in love and faith. And only the Lord can know which of us have the Devil inside us. Let the Lord's true judgments be upon us all! Not the false judgments of men."

Whispers rumbled through the benches and a nervousness filled Caroline's heart. Skirts and boots shuffled with the murmurs. Reverend Dane's words rang of truth inside her, and yet she could hear that not all had agreed with the reverend. The fervor of Salem threatened to burn through the congregations of Andover.

When at long last the meeting was over, Caroline stood. John leaned against a wall in the back of the meetinghouse with his arms crossed. A deep frown marred his face.

"Caroline?" Rebecca Ballard approached with her youngest daughter clutching her hand at her side. "Your John spoke to mine. He said you needed a ride home after the services?"

"I — " Caroline looked over Rebecca's shoulder to where John stood in the back. Rebecca's husband and brother-in-law stood beside him. When he noticed Rebecca standing beside her, he nodded his head and left, without offering a parting affection. She took a long breath. "I would be much obliged, yes. I know you have plenty to fill your hands already."

"It is no trouble. The boys can hitch one of our horses to your cart and drive you home."

Rebecca's seven other children gathered around her with expectant faces, their desire not to tarry a moment longer than needed evident in their approach. Caroline imagined herself in Rebecca's place and a deep twisted yearning to know such a reality filled her. Rebecca's children tittered and fussed but obeyed as she imparted a moment of her love to each of them. Caroline only had such moments when she knelt at her children's graves.

"I have changed my mind." She had never expressly gone against John's wishes. Her heart sped up as each word left her mouth. "I think I will walk home instead. Have the boys return for the cart when they can."

Rebecca's face furrowed in confusion. "Walk? To Salem?"

“No. I wish to stay in Andover until John’s return.”

3

# THE TOWN, SEPTEMBER 1685, SEVEN YEARS PRIOR

*Pain twisted inside of Caroline. "Johhnn," she moaned as it crested again. "Please. Make it stop. Make it stop."*

*John flitted around her, hovering but never touching, his comfort always just out of reach. "What can I do? Tell me what to do."*

*She didn't know what to tell him. It had to be the baby. Memory told her it was. Still, her mind fought against the logic. It wasn't time. It wasn't due until February. A warmth bloomed between her legs, the wetness sticking first to her shift, then running into her stockings.*

*John's eyes widened and his feet stumbled from drink as his gaze focused upon the floor. "What – Caroline, you're bleeding!"*

*Caroline cried out as the pains began their ascent again. It hadn't hurt this bad when she'd lost the previous baby this early. It hadn't hurt this bad when she'd birthed their firstborn son. Why did it hurt so now? She sobbed as she reached for a stool, the wall, the bed – anything to hold onto. "It hurts. Please, John. It hurts. Please, please."*

*His footsteps thundered upon the stairs. Clashes of glass and muttered oaths carried into the room.*

*Caroline focused on the clumsy sounds. On any sound that could distract.*

*"Here, drink this." John shoved a bottle into her hands and helped her guide its mouth to her lips.*

*She swallowed past the bitterness, gulping more than she would normally consume. Beer was not her drink of choice as it often disagreed with her. But perhaps the alcohol would numb the pain.*

*She finished a third swallow and John took the bottle to his lips, drinking twice as much as her. Anger flared inside her. How could he give in to his fears so readily when she needed him?*

*"Give it back." She wrestled the bottle away from him. His shocked expression gave her the slightest satisfaction until nausea hit and she vomited upon the floor. The repeated retching brought her to her knees.*

*Beer, bile, and blood mixed together at her feet. Her pains renewed their assault. Caroline was past caring for her cleanliness and she moaned as she curled up on the floor with it all.*

*"Oh God," John sobbed. "Oh God, oh God. I can't do this again. Don't die, Caroline. Don't die."*

*Another voice pierced through her pains. "Get up and fetch a bucket of water and rags, John Choate, before you become completely useless with drink."*

*Caroline couldn't open her eyes while the pain peaked. But she recognized the woman's voice. Their neighbor. Bridget Bishop. Soft tsks from the older woman's mouth comforted her ears.*

*"Come here, child."*

*Her sobs renewed as Bridget's hands worked with grace and efficiency, stripping Caroline of her soiled garments. "The baby?"*

*Bridget pressed wet rags across Caroline's face and skin. "It will pass soon, Goody Choate. The Lord wishes to claim it for himself."*

*"It hurts."*

*"Yes, I imagine it does." Bridget tucked Caroline's hair behind her ear. "I could hear your cries across the orchard. It is a wonder the rest of Salem didn't hear you too."*

*"But why? Why does this keep happening? Why does it hurt so much?"*

*"Some hurt more than others. There is no rhyme or reason to it." Bridget took Caroline's hand in her own. "Squeeze my hand when the pains come again. We'll get you through this."*

*She nodded and kept a firm grip upon Bridget's proffered hand as the older woman helped her pull on a new shift and climb into bed. The quilt would soil, but it would hopefully protect the newly stuffed mattress John had bought to celebrate.*

*"John?" Where was John?*

*Bridget glanced over her shoulder to a spot on the floor and Caroline followed her gaze. John was passed out with an empty bottle in his hand. Several others he had emptied before Bridget's arrival sat in condemnation about the room.*

*"He's not much use to you anymore, Goody Choate." Her face scrunched up in disgust. "Men rarely have the constitution for such things."*

*Caroline's gaze lingered upon John as her heart went out to him. The same darkness that often cornered her in this house had found him in this moment. "I never would have guessed he would act like this. He was not like this with the others."*

*"What number is this for you?"*

*"Three."*

*"There will be more. God willing, there will be more. It is a miracle you got through the first two without anyone else. But you shouldn't need to rely on your husband so much, Goody Choate. There are plenty of us in Salem when the midwife cannot be called. We may not always get along, but we do know how to serve one another as the Lord intended."*

*The beginnings of another wave of pain hit her with a force that made her hiss through her teeth. Bridget squeezed her hand as a reminder and Caroline squeezed back.*

*"How much longer?" she asked between shattered breaths.*

*"A couple hours, maybe more. Maybe a day or*

*two. There's no telling how long or how painful. But it will end."*

*Tears streamed down Caroline's face once more. "How can it end when I don't even know how it begins?"*

*"Because it always ends, Goody Choate. It always ends. For all of us."*

*After three days of intermittent pain and bleeding, Caroline gave birth to her firstborn daughter. Mercy Choate breathed for twelve hours before joining her two older brothers, John Jr. and Josiah Choate, in death.*

## THE TOWN, MAY 9TH, 1692

Almost three weeks passed without a word from John. Two weeks more than Caroline expected.

She watched the road with deep concern after the first week, slowly filling the pantry and larder of the Andover house as her stay prolonged first one day, and then another. Her worries for John kept her hands busy, and her children, buried at the edge of the property, kept her heart full. Under such attentions, land and home came alive with the last stirrings of spring. Then John's note found her there, requesting her to meet him at the Salem Town meetinghouse on the 9th day of May.

Thirteen more people had been arrested for witchcraft in John's absence. Their names brought the total of the accused to twenty-five. And each name brought the fear of the Devil closer to Caroline's front steps in Andover. What fever had seized upon so many in Salem that they should accuse and be accused of such eternally condemning acts?

It was with these thoughts that Caroline crossed the threshold of Salem Town's meetinghouse once more, to another examination being conducted inside.

"You were in attendance at the services in

Boston and Charlestown, yet you did not partake of the sacraments at either?"

Caroline stilled at the words, though they were not directed at her. The esquire Hathorne sat in the judge's place, and a new accused stood tall at the front, his head unbowed. It was the Reverend George Burroughs, Salem Village's previous minister. She had known him to be true to his faith and compassionate with the troubled residents when he had resided here, despite their ill treatment of him. The shocking image of him before the judge made her forget her worries for John for a moment.

"Not with those particular congregations, no," Reverend Burroughs said.

"Had you taken it anywhere? When was your last full communion?"

"It has been so long, I hardly remember."

Caroline scanned the large group gathered to hear the examination. John was near the front, and he turned when she entered. She would have to go to him despite the examination being already under way.

"You have many children who are not baptized, do you not?"

Reverend Burroughs clenched his jaw. "Yes."

"Is it not your duty as a minister and a father to see to their salvation?"

“It is one I do not take lightly.”

“And yet, your children remain unbaptized. Is this not true?”

Reverend Burroughs paused, clearly conflicted in the answer he knew he must give. “All but the eldest, yes.”

Silence filled Caroline’s ears as she skirted around the room to her husband’s side. No one but John had noticed her. They were all transfixed upon the unthinkable – that a minister was at the center of the Devil’s work.

“George Burroughs, you have also been accused of calling upon the Devil during your journey here, casting a spell of thunder and blue lightning.”

“There was a fierce storm.”

“And you were the only man who was not afeared.”

Reverend Burroughs’s face hardened. “Men with a conscience of innocence never fear the judgments of God.”

Caroline sat upon the wooden bench next to John as Hathorne banged his fists against the pulpit. The sound made her jump and John pulled her closer, lacing his fingers with hers and placing them upon his lap.

“The Devil has given you physical strength beyond human capabilities,” Hathorne said. “No doubt he has also given you the means to withstand any fears."

"I declare to you I am innocent of all accusations of witchcraft. Nor am I a conjurer."

The words of both men were final; the judgment passed before it was spoken.

"George Burroughs. With these testimonies and accounts given before us, we commit thee with charges of witchcraft."

Murmurs broke through the crowd as they dispersed. They had seen twenty-five examinations like this before, and yet the verdict was still a shock.

John shook his head beside Caroline. "It is a shame these examinations should extend to ministers. But men are not God."

"No, they are not." And yet, she dared not believe that this man, the Reverend George Burroughs, could be persuaded by the Devil to such acts. She turned to John and caught the smell of the road still upon him. "What was the nature of your business, that it detained you for so long?"

John nodded to where Reverend Burroughs had been taken away. "I had to make a trip up to Maine to help retrieve him."

Caroline's mind emptied with shock. "You arrested Reverend Burroughs?"

"No, that honor was done by the constable. But they needed help bringing him all the way back to

Salem."

"But why?"

"He is a very strong man, Caroline. I know it was some time ago, but you must remember from when they lived here. And I had just successfully taken in Susannah Martin from Amesbury –"

"Susannah Martin? The widow who was examined a few days ago?"

"Yes, yes," John said as his body leaned into hers, pressing beside her on the bench. "She has been suspected of witchcraft for some time now. You cannot be truly surprised of her arrest."

Disapproval on the old woman's behalf budded inside her. "She is argumentative, yes, much like Bridget Bishop. But she is just a poor widow. She has nothing and no one, John. Surely, she is not a witch."

"Caroline, she was accused of it twenty years ago. And not once, but twice. Who's to say she isn't? One of their arrests is sure to rid your body of its curse."

They had discussed such a possibility before and while she could not discount it, her mind could not fathom any of the accused wishing such a thing upon her. "But John, such accusations – these are people's souls! Surely they would not all participate in such acts. It would damn them to hell."

"And yet, some have already confessed. The

slave, Tituba, for one. Are they not to be believed? Lying would damn them too. Why would these people trade one sin for another when the punishment is the same? No. It is more likely that those who have committed one, have committed the other, for their punishment in hell cannot be doubled. Only a trial will tell if those who deny it speak the truth."

Caroline's displeasure at John's actions spun with doubt. Lying was a sin just as grievous as witchcraft. But then, who was to be believed? The motives behind these accusations could not be greed, for many who had been arrested held little in the temporal scope. And it could not be from any prejudices against women, for many men had been arrested as well. Could his words be right? Was it sin, and sin alone that determined the accusations awarded to each soul?

John squeezed her hand, pulling her attention back to his side. "We all have our secrets. And I have not asked you yours so that you do not have to choose condemnation for yourself." His gaze was filled with censure. He must have learned of her decision not to return to Salem.

"I have been staying at the house in Andover," she rushed to say. "I did not return to Salem Town like you wished me to. I was too frightened, John. You must realize that. And with recent events, I could not do so without you."

They were alone now within the meetinghouse, and John kissed her forehead. "See how much better it feels to confess than to try and hide away the truth? We cannot conquer what we do not confess."

Caroline nodded. But she did not believe him. And for the first time, his affections soured inside her.

# 4

## THE VILLAGE, JULY 1686, SIX YEARS PRIOR

*Caroline knocked on the Parrises' door. She fought to keep her eyes focused upon it. There was no harm in her desires. It was a simple request. Yet her heart pounded and her mind screamed for her to run. To not seek this thing that would only torture her once more. It would only add to the echoes in their Salem home.*

*But if it worked? If it worked — oh, John would be filled with such joy.*

*The door creaked and Caroline closed her linen kerchief tighter around her despite the summer heat. The Parrises' youngest, Betty, answered the door. The small child held it open at a crack.*

*Caroline gave her a tentative smile. "Is the slave, Tituba, about?"*

*Betty stared at Caroline without speaking, then nodded. The family was new to Salem and still under negotiations for Mr. Samuel Parris to become the new minister of the Village. The Village's previous ministers, Reverend George Burroughs and Reverend Deodat Lawson, had repeatedly run into troubles concerning pay, but Samuel Parris would soon be the first ordained minister Salem had ever had and there was hope he would take the residents in hand where the others could not. He was a strict but knowledgeable man, from what she had gathered.*

*It was likely four-year-old Betty did not recognize Caroline from their previous meetings. Her heart went out to the child with her beautiful wide eyes and fat-filled cheeks. If their first son, Josiah, had lived he would have been the same age as Betty. Would he have had a similar look? She could almost imagine him standing beside her now, with his tiny fingers curling around her own as they visited the people of Salem.*

*"Oh, Goody Choate. Good morning." Betty's mother, Elizabeth Parris, opened the front door a little wider.*

*Caroline stepped inside. "I've not come to trouble you, Mistress Parris. I only wished to speak to your slave, Tituba, if I may."*

*Elizabeth Parris placed a hand on her back, supporting her swollen belly. "Certainly. Tituba is in the kitchen."*

*Caroline left for the kitchen before her jealousy could grow. It was true that Elizabeth was the prettiest woman in Salem, but that was not the reason she felt an undeniable envy each time they conversed.*

*The kitchen was hot, magnifying the season's natural heat in its enclosed space. Tituba's long black hair was coming undone beneath her coif as she worked over the fire. She was a younger woman, closer to Caroline's own age, and her shorter stature allowed her to work without stooping.*

*She turned her head easily at Caroline's entrance. "Mistress."*

*Caroline nodded and found her doubts resurfacing now that she was in the company of the Parrises' slave. Many of the wealthier residents in the Massachusetts Bay Colony owned slaves. There was nothing forbidding it. But even as John's status bloomed within Salem, he refused to buy one.*

*"It doesn't feel right," he told Caroline one night after she had asked, "owning another person. I'll not begrudge any man who wishes to improve his circumstances that way, but I'll have no part in it."*

*John's refusal had left her with little experience in dealing with slaves. How did one speak to a slave? Did she sit or stand when in their presence? Should she wait until Tituba was done with her work before issuing her request? Should she offer her words as a request, or a command?*

*An older girl, about nine years of age, with matching black hair and copper skin entered the kitchen behind Caroline. "Here are the onions, Mama."*

*"Thank you, child." Tituba glanced at Caroline again. "Violet, please help Mistress to a chair. There should be one behind the table."*

*Violet obeyed without hesitation and soon Caroline found herself sitting before the fire as Tituba kissed the top of Violet's head. Tituba ushered the child away before continuing her work.*

*"Now, how can I help you, Mistress?"*

*Tituba spoke in such lilting tones, dropping sounds and emphasizing others, almost like a song. She did not hold the same light-colored features as Elizabeth, but it was clear that she was a beauty of her own, even under her humbler clothes. It seemed Samuel Parris wished to surround himself with things of beauty. Caroline sat in appreciation for a moment as the sounds of Tituba's voice washed over her.*

*"I – forgive me, but you are of the native tribes, are you not?"*

*"Yes. Though not of the ones that trouble you here, Mistress, with their continual raids. I am from lands much farther south."*

*"But you are not a Christian?"*

*Tituba paused her work and met Caroline's gaze. "No. I am not like you, Mistress. Even though I have since believed, you know that my position as a slave prevents me from becoming so."*

*Caroline nodded, dismissing the tension creeping into Tituba's voice. "I have heard that the natives use remedies – ways to cure ailments." She clutched at her empty middle as the fervor and fear of her desires made her voice shake. "They can make things whole where our beliefs cannot."*

*Tituba's gaze dropped to Caroline's hands. The understanding within Tituba's eyes spurred her boldness.*

*"Tell me you know of such practices? Please."*

*Tituba's spine stiffened, and thanks to Caroline's seated position, the shorter slave woman looked down upon her with great censure. "You think because I am different than you, Mistress, that somehow I can save you? That it is my duty to give you benevolence when your god cannot?"*

*Caroline's eyes widened as she realized her assumptions. "No, I only hoped – please, I do not know who else to go to."*

*"I am a woman, no more knowledgeable than you. If you want knowledge, you should seek someone much older than you and I. Someone with experience. I had Violet when I myself was barely more than a child. And now none grow inside me. Do you not think, if I knew of some substance to cure me, I would have used it? Some spell to chant so that my husband and I could be blessed with one of our own?"*

*"I am sorry," Caroline whispered. Her shoulders slumped as they were once again burdened by ache and relief. She wiped away a tear that threatened to run down her cheek.*

*Tituba sighed. "How many have you lost, Mistress?"*

*"Four." Her fourth pregnancy had passed after less time than the others. Another boy. Oliver Choate. Caroline had barely felt the physical pains. Her heart had numbed itself upon the first signs of her impending loss. She hadn't even told John he was to be congratulated. Now there was nothing to celebrate. She hadn't let herself believe there would be.*

*Tituba patted her hands. The gesture was one of pity and comfort. It was so small, it only highlighted the other side of the great blackening fear that forever approached Caroline. A fear that this childlessness – this loneliness she felt in her womanhood – had been predetermined by God for her future.*

## THE VILLAGE, MAY 31ST, 1692

By the end of May, nine more persons had been arrested. Thirty-five people in three months. The knowledge that John had facilitated the speed of those arrests inspired a new unease that grew inside Caroline's heart. Within their Salem home, she suffered in silence during the day. But when the unease awakened her memories once again, her screams were added to their nights.

She had spoken no words against John's actions in the weeks that followed his confession. But that had been before today's examination. Before her dear friend, Martha Carrier, walked through the door, escorted by Rebecca Ballard's husband, the constable of Andover.

Her eyes widened. She turned and leaned in her seat, trying to get Martha's attention. But Martha would meet the eyes of no one in the room as she took her place before Hathorne. The weight of John's hand upon her thigh commanded Caroline to remain in her seat and to sit forward. She turned to him instead.

"Oh John, what have you done?" Her words hissed upon a shaky whisper. "Please tell me this was not your doing."

"I was not the only one who condemned her. She has been chanting curses for far too long. Too many in Andover have. You will see. Soon, none of them will hurt you anymore."

The hatred spewing from his eyes at their dearest neighbor in Andover stunned Caroline. The room narrowed around her. Her heartbeat pulsed in her ears.

"What do you say to this you are charged with?"

Hathorne's words jolted Caroline out from her shock. She had missed the opening of the examination.

Martha Carrier's gaze bored into Hathorne. If she were a pistol and he were a deer, she would have had him with a head shot. "I have not done it."

The same girls who had accused the other thirty-five cried out. "She looks upon the black man!"

"What black man is that?" Hathorne directed his question to Martha.

"I know none."

Several girlish cries of pain proclaimed to being pricked. One claimed again that Martha did look upon the black man.

Hathorne ignored the pain-filled cries. "What black man did you see?"

Martha's jaw tightened. "I saw no black man but your own presence."

Several in the crowd gasped. Caroline's own heart jumped at her friend's impertinence.

Hathorne's authoritative calm cracked beneath Martha's unyielding stare. "Can you look upon them?" He flung his arm to the girls gathered as her accusers. They fell down in obscene cries and agonies. "Can you look upon these and not knock them down?"

Martha did not avert her gaze. "They will dissemble if I look upon them. I have looked upon none but you since I came into the room."

"I see them!" One of the girls cried, still in a trance upon the floor. "Thirteen specters!"

The other girls followed.

"The same thirteen that she has killed in Andover!"

"There they are!"

"She killed them!"

Caroline held her breath as Martha's face slipped into one of sorrow. Everyone knew of the thirteen people the girls referred to. It was the thirteen that had died of smallpox, including Martha's father, her two brothers, a sister and brother-in-law, two nephews, and two of her own children.

"They have her now." John's whisper crawled up the side of Caroline's neck, reminding her body of past pleasures and turning them into pains. She did not want him anywhere near her person. But he was her husband. She should not feel such recoiling with him.

"You lie!" Martha cried out at last, the words retching from her mouth as deep hurts and doubts played across her once composed face. "I am the one who was wronged," she whispered at last.

Her last words were barely uttered before tortured cries were taken up once again by the girls. Their flailing upon the floor grew violent, and Hathorne called out at last to the constable for him and his men to tie Martha up, hand and foot, and remove her from the room. John stood as Hathorne finished his command.

"John, no!" Caroline reached for his arm. But she had waited a moment too long while he had not.

John glanced once at her before joining the other men. Amid the girls' writhing screams, they bound Martha, then dragged her out of the meetinghouse. Caroline's gaze darted around the room as they did so. Where was Martha's husband, Thomas? Her sons, Richard and Andrew? Where was someone who would help her? Would no one speak up?

The room quieted as each girl finished her torments. The silence clawed at Caroline's throat. Then the proceedings continued as the accusing girls adopted an air of contented ease.

Hathorne shuffled his papers, then pulled out a

quill and scribbled a note. “Martha Carrier.” He addressed his recited words to no one, as Martha was not present. “Upon hearing and seeing with our own eyes the stated evidence, we commit thee with charges of witchcraft.”

His pronouncement echoed through the room and everyone there served as a witness complicit in Martha’s charges, including Caroline. Nausea engulfed her at the thought. She could not move as the others departed. What had she just done?

“Come. This day is not over.” John had returned for Caroline. He took her hands in his and she fought with the discomforting urge to recoil from his touch.

She shook her head. “No, please, John. I cannot. I cannot witness anymore.”

“The governor has set up a court at last to hear these cases.”

“Please, John. Do not make me.”

“Bridget Bishop’s trial will be first.”

“You know I cannot do this.”

“We must go to Salem Town.”

“Please.”

Caroline’s final plea broke in her throat. John crouched before her, bringing his face level with hers as he searched for her thoughts. His brow furrowed. She looked away from his gaze with shame.

"Very well. You can stay at home, if you think it best. But I must go and see what punishment is decided for our neighbor."

Their neighbor. Bridget Bishop. Martha Carrier. Even Susannah Martin, George Burroughs, and all the others. Were they not their neighbors? They had not truly wished her any ill will, witches or not. And yet she had not spoken out on any of their behalf. How could she ever face any of them again?

Caroline allowed John to take her outside as these thoughts consumed her into oblivion. Only the weight of his hands chained around her own carried her through the street.

## ANDOVER, JULY 1686, SIX YEARS PRIOR

*Caroline's visit with the slave Tituba weighed upon her happiness as John stopped their cart at the Allens' house in Andover.*

*John helped her down, then pulled her hands up to his chest. "You have had a cloud of darkness about you since we left." He kissed her knuckles with reverence. "Tell me, what troubles you?"*

*Release bubbled at the surface of her emotions. "Am I a bad person, John?"*

*His hand caressed her cheek with a sudden fierce protection. "No, Caroline." He hushed her and wiped the tears from her eyes before they could fall. "How could you think such things?"*

*"Why has God taken our children? Why does he allow my womb to fill only to leave my arms empty? My heart cannot take it anymore, John."*

*His kisses littered her face as he attempted to soothe her. "They are with God. Be happy that they are with him and think of them no more."*

*A throat cleared behind them. John looped his arm around the small of Caroline's back as he turned them to their unexpected audience.*

*"John. Caroline." Goodman Allen's smile suggested he hadn't noticed Caroline's tears. But the twinkle in his eye said he hadn't missed John's kisses. "You've made good time today. My daughter*

*and son-in-law just arrived from Billerica."*

*A man who towered above John and Goodman Allen stepped forward. "Thomas Carrier," he said as he shook John's hand. "This here's my wife, Martha, and our youngest, Sarah."*

*Martha pushed past her giant husband, a small toddler on her hip. "You must be the Choates. My father has told us much about you."*

*John chuckled. "All good things, I hope?"*

*"All good things, all good things." Goodman Allen waved John's jest away. "Martha, why don't you see to Goody Choate while Goodman Choate and I discuss our business. Thomas, you should come with us."*

*John squeezed Caroline's side before leaving with the men. Her eyes followed the bounce of Sarah's dark curls as Martha adjusted her on her hip.*

*"How long have you and Goodman Choate been married?"*

*Caroline forced her gaze to Martha's. "Near five years now."*

*Martha's hand came up as she turned a suspicious smile into a cough. She had seen John's kisses too then. "Thomas and I are the same way as you and Goodman Choate, though we've enjoyed twelve years now. We have six little ones to prove it. Our oldest, Richard, was born just two months after we married."*

*Caroline did not hide the shock in her eyes at Martha's confession.*

*Martha leaned in. "And we have another on the way. Don't tell Thomas. You're the first to know, Goody Choate."*

*"Oh. I, uh – I thank thee. That is wonderful news." Caroline's words rang hollow even to her own ears.*

*Martha's brow wrinkled and at last her gaze fell to Caroline's flat belly. Immediate understanding softened her eyes. "When was your last one?"*

*"Five months past. In February. John does not know." She had laid the boy in a basket, wrapped him in a quilt, and secured him outside in the orchard until the freezing temperatures had warmed enough to thaw the ground for his burial. John had not noticed her suffering. But he was sure to see the new grave eventually whenever they visited their Andover home.*

*"Then we are friends, already sharing secrets."*

*Martha's smile reached inside Caroline's shadows. And in her desperate want to not be left alone, she shared more than she would have with a stranger.*

*"I have not bled since. With the others everything went back to normal so fast. There has been no quickening, but do you think..."*

*Martha surveyed Caroline again. "It is hard to*

*tell. But it is possible. The baby would not be far grown if you were. Do you and Goodman Choate still find pleasure with each other during the night?"*

*Caroline blushed. Still, Martha seemed to wish for a spoken answer. "Yes. Though not as often as before. At least, not in the same manner."*

*Martha nodded. "Then it is likely your womb wishes to rest. You have asked much of it these past years, yes? The body needs time to strengthen, to renew. It will bleed again when it is ready. And then you must tell Goodman Choate that you are ready to have his son."*

## THE TOWN, JUNE 10TH, 1692

Bridget Bishop's trial was delayed until the second of June. Still, Caroline did not go to the trial. She did not witness the testimonies declared against the old woman. She did not see the violating examination of Bridget's naked body for the witch teats and dark marks upon her skin.

But she had heard everything as she laid sick in bed at the thought. At what John had done. At what she, Caroline, had done by allowing it. She heard through the condemning whispers of their neighbors and through John's own voice. Bridget Bishop was declared guilty. The punishment for witchcraft was decided. She would hang. All declared guilty would hang.

Caroline followed the executing procession across the North River on Bridge Street with John beside her. The crowd was large, and the cart carrying Bridget Bishop moved slow. The summer sun beat out the desire to speak. Even the children did not call out as they jostled around the cart. After a week of her melancholy, John had insisted Caroline come. The sleeve of his doublet scratched against her hand now as he escorted her up the hill.

The cart stopped at the top of Gallows Hill, below a tree where a single rope with a noose at the end was attached. The people of Salem gathered around: restless, fearful, and unable to look away.

"Bridget Bishop," the sheriff said. "As the condemned, you are allowed last words."

"Confess!" came a shout from the crowd, followed by another. "Confess, witch! Confess!"

Shouts turned into roars, and the sheriff's men were forced to push the most zealous away from the cart.

"I am no witch!" Bridget's shout mixed with the crowds. She set her jaw in a familiar defiant stare as the sheriff's men blindfolded her. Then they guided her, with her hands bound behind her back, to a ladder that had been placed next to the tree behind them.

John patted Caroline's hand as the men tied Bridget's legs together. Sickening dread pooled in Caroline's belly. But before she could cover her face, one of the men kicked the ladder out from Bridget's feet.

Shrieks mixed with cheers as Bridget dangled from the tree. Caroline's cry was lost in the noise and she stared as Bridget's body convulsed, fighting to live. Each movement made her stomach turn more upon itself. Minutes passed. Too many minutes. The rope had not caught the neck the way it was intended. It was not a strong enough grip to render the woman unconscious. Around Caroline, the crowd fought in their witness of Bridget's death. Those who had been against it were trapped between those who wished for it and the horror of the prolonged strangulation.

"John," Caroline pleaded in a whisper.

"It is almost finished."

Her hands shook beneath his. Her knees locked. Blood pounded in her temples. Bridget's body twitched.

*Thump.*

John shuffled his feet beside Caroline and she swayed into him, catching herself before she fell.

*Thump.*

Caroline's heart stopped. She pulled a hand free from John's grip and placed it against her belly.

*Thump. Thump.*

Her eyes widened. She glanced up at John with dread.

He looked down at her. "It is over, my dear."

"What?"

He nodded to where Bridget's body hung lifeless in the tree. They had pulled the cart underneath her once again. One of the sheriff's men cut Bridget's rope and the sound of her body hitting the wooden cart reverberated in perfect time inside Caroline.

*Thump.*

The men rolled the cart away and Caroline's

thoughts raced inside her mind. A child. She was with child. These were not the spectral movements of her lost children. Her hand had felt the quickening too. John would feel it if she pressed closer to him.

Oh, John. What was she to tell John?

His gaze traveled over her face with worry. "Are you unwell, Caroline? You have gone pale."

Her bleeding had come at irregular intervals for years now. And after the harrowing deaths of the twins, John had sought her company with the same irregularity. She could not recall the last time they had laid together as husband and wife. Yet somehow, a child had come to be within her womb.

"I-I am not sure," she said with complete honesty.

John's humor immediately shifted into careful efficiency. His touch was gentle but firm as he guided her down the hill. His glances were soft but assessing as they crossed the bridge over the North River. When he tried to pick her up, Caroline stopped him.

"I can walk."

"Are you quite certain? You look as if the very Devil has cursed you with sickness."

Caroline nodded.

"Was it Bridget Bishop? Did her specter curse you as we stood waiting for her death?"

"N...n-no," she stammered, horrified that his thoughts had again so quickly turned there.

"Was it one of the others?"

Caroline squeezed his arm as she shook her head. "No. It was no act of witchcraft. Please, John. Do not speak of such things."

John narrowed his eyes in displeasure, but he did not push it any further. "Very well. We are almost home."

Home. Her body braced for the memories of their Salem home, and for what the movements inside her would bring.

# 5

## THE TOWN, JUNE 1687, FIVE YEARS PRIOR

*Caroline had labored for eighteen hours before she felt the unbearable weight of crowning. Sweat from exhaustion and the summer heat flowed freely down the swollen curves of her body. She had long since stripped her bloodied petticoats and shift. It was still early for the child to come, and she feared a repeat of the past four pregnancies.*

*Martha wiped away the wetness from Caroline's face as she squatted in front of her. "You're almost there, Caroline. Just a little bit longer. The babe is ready. Push when I say. We must work with your body, not against it."*

*Caroline nodded, trusting Martha's words. She was past the point of making her own decisions. Her waters had broken while cleaning in the kitchen of their Salem home, the water from the bucket tricking her into believing it hadn't truly happened. But when John had found her doubled over in pain moments later, word was sent immediately to Andover.*

*Martha rode through the night astride her husband's fastest horse. Her wind-swept hair and rumpled skirts filled Caroline with guilt in the moment. But Martha had chided her sensibilities, reassuring her it was no hardship to help a friend.*

*There was no room for Caroline to feel guilt now. Only inevitability. The baby was coming.*

*She gripped the posters of the bed frame as her legs began to shake. Her low moan turned into a roar.*

*"Push!"*

*Caroline's body responded to Martha's command. Martha's hands moved from the small of her back to her entrance. She hardly felt Martha there though as the pressure built beyond belief, and then, a squelching movement of release as the baby slipped into this world.*

*Caroline reached below, meeting Martha's hands where they held the bundle. He was bigger than the others had been, but still too small. His body shook with rigidity as she pulled him to her chest.*

*"A boy." Tears escaped Caroline's eyes as she kissed the top of his head. "Samuel."*

*Martha's arms wrapped around her. "Let's get you two settled. See if he will take to the breast."*

*Caroline nodded. Martha's implied words rang over her head as she sat. He would need to eat if he were to have a chance at living.*

*They placed Samuel at Caroline's breast. She pleaded silent prayers as his mouth fought to coordinate the muscles needed to latch, swallow, and breathe.*

*"He's almost there," Martha said in a gentle*

*whisper. "Keep working at it and he'll get it."*

*Caroline nodded as tears swelled in her eyes again. Samuel. He was the son she had prayed for these past months, and at last, God had delivered.*

*Martha smoothed the top of Caroline's hair. "I'll go get John now. He should know he has a son."*

*Caroline shushed and swaddled the baby as she fought with her rising worries. Samuel continued to struggle as they waited for John and Martha's return. He pulled, suckled, released, and shook with tiny cries each time his hunger was left unsatisfied.*

*His attempts at Caroline's breast increased the pains inside her womb. She tried to push them from her mind, but the pains grew in intensity and then in frequency. Suddenly, the unbearable weight was at her entrance again.*

*"Martha!" she gasped. "Martha!"*

*The door of the bedroom swung open as Martha flew into the room. John followed behind her. Caroline's panic could not be restrained and she cried out as her pain crested again. Samuel's cries became muffled in her breast. She had clenched him against her too hard.*

*"John, take the baby." Martha pulled at the blanket covering Caroline's legs. Swaths of blood drenched through the mattress and blanket. Her eyes widened.*

*Samuel's cries grew more insistent.*

*Martha turned on John. "Take the baby out. Now. There is another."*

*John obeyed but hesitated at the door, his vulnerable eyes lingering over Caroline. "Another what?"*

*The reality of Martha's words sank into Caroline's mind. "Another baby!" She cried out as Martha helped her into position.*

*"Go, now!"*

*Martha grabbed Caroline's hands, and as the door shut she dropped her voice into a rushed whisper. "There has been too much blood already. Something has gone wrong. But I will see you through this, Caroline Choate. I swear before God you will survive. You will not leave your child motherless."*

*"You mean," Caroline fought for her words, "you mean children. There is another. A twin."*

*Martha didn't answer. Her hands worked furiously inside Caroline, creating a scraping pain. Blood continued to soak through the quilt and Martha's shirtsleeves. Caroline's heart pounded in her chest. Then at last Martha commanded. "Push!"*

*Caroline's body worked as before, pushing the baby through in a squelching movement with less time. Her vision blurred.*

*"A girl. It is a girl, Caroline. She lives." Martha's voice was fading fast.*

*"Rachel," Caroline whispered. Her lips moved to speak her daughter's name again, but no sound escaped. Rachel's tiny cries faded away as her vision went black.*

*When she woke, five days had passed. Her daughter, Rachel Choate, had lived for one day. Her son, Samuel Choate, had lived for three. John had sat with each as they wasted away without a wet nurse's breast, unable to provide what they or Caroline needed.*

*It took Caroline six weeks before she left her bed. And it was months more before John returned to hers.*

## THE TOWN, AUGUST 6TH, 1692

"Caroline?" The bed dipped as John sat beside her on the bed. "Here is more broth. And I have brought bread this time if you think you can stomach it."

Caroline shook her head. Her stomach was not sick because of the baby, not in the same way it had been with the others. But still her appetite had avoided her these past two months. John hovered as she sipped, frowning as he studied the evidence of sleepless nights under her eyes. She kept her gaze from finding his. She did not know if she could speak of it yet.

They had hanged five more women in July. And sixteen more were arrested – nine from Andover. All while Caroline's belly grew. Life for life; unequally exchanged.

The trials of six more were being conducted this week. John told Caroline this as she laid on their bed through it all, confined to their little house in Salem. She could see Gallows Hill through the window if she turned her head. She wouldn't though, not while John was here beside her. She looked at the scene often during the night, with the summer moonlight shattering through the hanging trees, playing the events of Bridget's death over and over in her mind as she fought against the nightmares that dripped their way into her waking moments.

"Thank you." She handed the bowl back to John. He checked her for fever once again. She let him each time, knowing his fingers would never find burning skin. It was something for him to do and he needed the purpose. He knew the cause of her malady. There was no hiding her swelling belly from him. Not when he helped her dress and undress each day. And not when he held her body against his each night.

John should have known Caroline's terror for himself. She had seen the moment in his eyes when his hands had found the quickening. Shock. Memory. Realization. Fear. They both knew what the movements meant. What they could not have. What they must endure once again. But then John spoke of witches and their fault in the loss of each child. Determination shadowed his face each time he left Caroline's side to arrest another.

John leaned over her and hesitated. "I must go now."

Caroline nodded. There was to be another trial today. Martha's trial. She would not attend though John had asked her to. He wanted her to sit beside him. But she could not. Whether it was because of the specters in the house, the trials of the town, or the guilt at her part in them, she could not say.

Dread kept her prisoner. It had stolen her appetite, her strength, her emotions, and her voice.

John left without his token kiss upon Caroline's forehead. Even with their recent distance, the loss of him added to the weight upon her heart.

She stared out at Gallows Hill. The green of the leaves would fade soon. It was summer now, but she had lived in the Massachusetts Bay Colony long enough to know their vibrancy would not last. Not when an equal vibrancy would burn through the trees in yellows, oranges, and reds come September.

They would hang Martha among those trees. Caroline had known it since the verdict of Bridget's trial. All of the accused would hang in those same trees where Bridget was executed. There was no stopping the sentences once they had begun. Caroline felt it in the air she breathed each day. It was a choking air that settled around her bones and threatened to bury her, far beneath her children.

And perhaps it would bury her. It would be a blessing to not have to live with her guilt – to not have to live with the madness of Salem, the madness of her mind, or the madness of her womb.

The child within her stirred. It was strong. Much stronger than the others. It fought against her ribs and hips, bruising her with fault.

*Thump.*

*Thump. Thump.*

Caroline brought her hand up over her belly, applying a counterpressure to the child's movements. The bed creaked beneath her.

*Thump. Thump.*

A knocking sounded on the back door, polite at first, then repeated with force.

Caroline groaned as she sat up and swung her feet over the side of the bed. Dizziness took her at once and she clutched at the blankets. The movement made a memory flash before her. Wetness. Stickiness. Red, blooming between her legs too soon. She could see it now. She could feel it now. It was there, right there in the bed. Sobs caught in her throat.

*Thump. Thump.*

The persistent knocking echoed inside of Caroline and pulled her from her imaginings. There was no blood nor wetness upon the bed. There was someone at the door. She needed to answer the door.

She hobbled through the halls, her legs shaking with weakness and disuse. She clutched the door handle, resting a part of her weight upon it before opening it for her visitors. Thomas Carrier and his youngest daughter, Hannah, stood outside in the shadow-less midday light.

"Caroline." Thomas Carrier tipped his hat in

greeting, but his actions were rushed. Agitated. Bereft.

"Thomas." She clenched the handle tighter. "Come in. Come in."

Thomas guided Hannah through the door with one hand on her back and the other holding her small hand. The three-year-old's eyes were puffy either from crying or from a lack of sleep. Or both. The two of them would have had to have left Andover during the night to make it here at such an hour. Crumpled clothes and dirty faces confirmed they had yet to stop and make themselves presentable for Martha's trial.

*Thump. Thump. Thump.*

Thomas's eyes fell on Caroline's swollen belly. Surprise lit his face, then pity. They had never spoken about it, but he knew enough of her troubles to know what this pregnancy meant for her. Everyone in Andover and Salem knew of her history. And everyone had learned not to speak of it, silencing her hurt before it could become theirs. Thomas's knowing gaze made her want to return to the emptiness of her bed. But she could not ignore Martha's child.

"Let me get you something to wash with." She balled her hands into fists, clenching at the shakes still threatening within them. "Or a drink? Are you hungry?" She turned toward the cupboards. John had offered her bread earlier. Perhaps there was still a bit left.

Thomas sat Hannah at the table. But he did not join her. Instead his hulking frame filled the space of the kitchen with a nervous energy.

"I've, uh – I've come to see about posting bail for the children. I wouldn't ask it of ye, Caroline, if I had known. But I've no one else in Salem Town to turn to."

*Thump. Thump.*

Caroline pushed against the child within her, smoothing over the taut skin of her belly. She shook her head. "You know I cannot offer you money, Thomas. John – "

"It wouldn't be money, no. I wouldn't ask that of ye. I need someone to look after Hannah. The lass is too wee to be at home alone, and I cannot abide the thought of having her near the trials. They've already arrested Richard, Andrew, Thomas Jr., and Sarah. I don't want them to press for Hannah too."

They had taken Martha's children in with her, all in hopes that it would move her to confess. She hadn't broken yet. But she might if little Hannah were brought to her in chains too.

"You've come to post bail? Have they charged the children with crimes?" Caroline faced the table with the loaf of bread in hand. Hannah's little feet tapped against the table as her fingers picked at the splintered wood near a knot.

Thomas cleared his throat. "They strung the boys up by their heels and questioned them until their noses bled. Richard – Richard confessed. He says he had to in order to stop them. Didn't want them to hurt the younger ones anymore, let alone Sarah. The other three confessed after him."

"To witchcraft?"

Thomas nodded.

Caroline found a rag and a bucket of water. She crouched before Hannah. Thomas's older children would know what they had cost themselves with their confession. Only time would tell if they could live with the guilt of their damnation. She wiped away at Hannah's face until the skin turned pink again.

Familiar heavy footsteps approached the front of the house. Caroline paused. An undercurrent of fear flowed beneath little Hannah's stillness. It was John.

He stood at the entrance of the kitchen, the top of his head brushing the frame of the doorway, though he still did not fill the space the way Thomas did. John's gaze traveled over the older man, then Hannah, before finding Caroline still crouched in front of the girl. He scratched his beard. Caroline's shoulders tensed.

"What's this?" John stepped closer to her. "What

are you doing out of bed?"

Caroline dipped the rag into the bucket and cleaned Hannah's hands. "Thomas needs our help. We'll be looking after Hannah until the trials can be sorted."

"I'll not have one of them living in this house. They are witches, Caroline. Every last one of them. Their mother is the Queen of Hell and has taught them everything she knows."

A chair scraped against the wooden floorboards as Thomas crossed the room with one step. The bucket at Caroline's feet sloshed and wetness soaked through the front of her petticoats. She fought to breathe as her mind flared with memory. Her body braced for pain. She clenched her teeth.

"I'll not have you speak ill of my wife, John Choate. Nor my children." Thomas's voice growled through Caroline's memories. "How can you say such things after all our years of friendship?"

"They are the truth."

"They are lies!"

"Stop it!" Caroline's raised voice shocked everyone, including herself. She had never raised her voice to John, not in all their ten years of marriage. She took a deep breath, her hands shaking as she tried to rid herself of the past. "We will care for Hannah as our own. It is our Christian duty."

John had no answer. Whether shock or guilt rendered him speechless, it did not matter to Caroline in that moment. She used his silence to press her advantage.

"I will take the girl back to Andover. She need not stay in this cursed house with the people of Salem. You may come if you wish. Thomas will drive us back if you do not." She glanced at Thomas, who nodded. "But you will not stop me, John Choate."

Anger, mixed with hurt, brimmed at the surface of John's face. "I came back to see if you had changed your mind about coming to the trial. But clearly you have not."

The slam of the front door hit Caroline in a moment of heavy regret. They were man and wife. After all these years, she had formed so much of her identity around him. But these witches were spinning a divide between them she feared they would never cross. John's footsteps stomped away from the house and faded into the distance.

*Thump. Thump. Thump.*

# 6

## THE TOWN, MAY 1690, TWO YEARS PRIOR

*Caroline held the lifeless infant against her chest. A girl. No bigger than her hands. Martha Choate. Her seventh child.*

*Caroline's friend, Martha Carrier, the child's namesake, still lay in bed in Andover. The smallpox had come through and all of Martha's family had caught it. They had battled it in isolation for months without a promise any of them would make it. When Caroline learned of her pregnancy, she vowed that should this child be a girl, she would name her for Martha. For surely one of that name would have to live.*

*Word had reached Caroline and John only an hour after her delivery. Martha would recover. The tears that escaped Caroline were filled with shameful relief. For so long she had wanted a child. It had been a dream she had fought for. For John, and for herself. But faced now with little Martha's death, and the threat of smallpox in neighboring Andover, Caroline was glad the child had not survived. She was glad her friend had been spared. She was glad that she would not have to face the worry of an infant stricken with smallpox. And she was ashamed of her gladness.*

*John had left Caroline to deliver the baby alone.*

*He was more trouble within the birthing room than outside it. But she hadn't needed any help. This was her seventh. And although it had been early, there had been no surprises. Her body had worked as it should, its pains increasing with purpose before bearing down upon the barrier of this world that separated creation and life.*

*But what her body could not control was the passage each of her children had taken from life into death. Caroline stared out the window of her bedroom to where she could see a hill, with trees full of fresh summer leaves, cresting at the edge of Salem Town. She would never be able to give a child a life as vibrant as the leaves upon that hill.*

*Caroline placed baby Martha upon the bed. She pressed her hands upon the tiny face, smoothing out the skin, before gently pulling upon her nose in the way that it would grow had she survived. Then she wrapped Martha within the quilt bloodied from her birth, covering the child's face only after her arms and legs had been straightened and swaddled close. Caroline placed the bundle in a basket by the door. It would be used to transport the baby to her grave at their Andover home. Then, Caroline crawled back into her bed and at last, she welcomed rest.*

## ANDOVER, AUGUST 18TH, 1692

Caroline's hands grasped the small shovel as it bit into the dirt. The ground was still soft from summer, and the infant-sized hole appeared without any strenuous effort.

The day was just beginning. Little Hannah Carrier played with her doll beside Caroline, dipping its feet in the fresh pile of dirt between spurts of conversation and sweet smiles. Shades of green lingered in the quaking leaves above them and highlighted the innocent twinkle in Hannah's eyes. Caroline's pains hadn't begun. But they would soon. And she would go through everything again without John. She had not heard from him since that day in Salem, almost two weeks ago. She had not expected to. Her sorrow at their separation was still new.

Thomas appeared in the distance and when Hannah saw him she squealed before tossing her doll aside. It fell into the fresh grave. Thomas gave Hannah a kiss before setting her on her feet and encouraging her to return to her play.

"I'm off to Salem now."

Caroline brushed the dirt from her hands on her apron. "Will you return after tomorrow?"

Thomas shook his head. "I've still got four children in that prison." His gaze found where

Hannah's doll lay and he winced. "You haven't told Hannah about..."

"No. I've said nothing of Martha, though she still cries for her each night."

Thomas nodded. "If you could keep her just a bit longer —"

"It is no trouble, Thomas." His gaze fell on her protruding belly and Caroline pressed her hands around it. "Having Hannah here will not change what is to come for this babe."

"Martha wishes she were here to help. I told her of your news after the trial."

Tears welled in Caroline's eyes. "I wish she were here too. I'm so sorry, Thomas. I never thought that John — "

"You are not to blame for his actions. And in truth, I am sure someone else would have done the same if he had not. The accusations in Salem are rampant and unchecked. It was only a matter of time before the Devil's work reached us here in Andover."

"Do you think it will run its course through us as well?"

"It's hard to say. Martha was contentious, we both know that. But she kept our family together through the smallpox. And I can keep us together through what's to come. I'll not stop until my petitions are heard."

Caroline nodded. “Safe travels, Thomas.”

Thomas turned to go, but they had lingered too long in their conversation and Hannah had returned, her play forgotten.

“Da.” Hannah’s little arms reached for him again.

Caroline stepped between them. “I’ve got her, Thomas.”

“No, it’s all right.” The giant man scrunched down to his daughter’s height. Hannah wrapped her arms around his neck and buried her face into his gray whiskers. Thomas squeezed her as he blinked away his tears. “You’ll mind Goody Choate, won’t you, Hannah dear? Help her with her chores, like Ma and Sarah taught you.”

Hannah’s voice flitted through his embrace. “Is Ma coming home?”

Thomas blinked harder. “No. Ma will be with God soon. She’ll not be coming back this way. Though she loves you very much.” He gave Hannah a kiss, then ushered her into Caroline’s keeping. “I’ll be back. Take care of Goody Choate while I am gone.”

Hannah frowned, but she did not cry. The crying, Caroline knew, would come later that night, when both of them would fight the sorrows that plagued them.

Martha was hanged the next morning for

witchcraft beside four men. Caroline heard it told that Reverend Burroughs, one of the hanged, recited the Lord's Prayer in its entirety before the noose was placed around his neck. It was a feat that could not be done by witches or any associates of the Devil. But even that proof did not stop the executions, or the arrests that followed.

# 7

## ANDOVER, OCTOBER 10TH, 1692

*Thump.*

*Thump. Thump. Thump.*

Caroline laid still, her body too worn to move after waking so early. Between the late-night cries of Hannah Carrier, the waking terrors of Caroline's dreams, and the early morning movements of the child within her, her body ached for sleep. Her mind pleaded for oblivion.

In the six weeks that had passed after Martha Carrier's death, forty-four more persons were arrested for witchcraft. Thirty-one of them were people of Andover. Caroline had no doubt of John's hand in their arrest. Most were forced to confess, like the Carrier children were, as the fire of accusations ran unchecked. Two weeks prior, on September 22nd, that fire burned the brightest as eight men and women were hanged.

*Thump. Thump.*

She dared not move while Hannah still slept. For two months, Caroline had waited for her pains. And when each day ended without them, she smothered her hopes with a blanket of the nightmares that had followed her from Salem. They hadn't been as severe here in Andover, but still they persisted as her pregnancy lingered. Hannah had stayed with her the entire time, blessedly seeming to sleep through Caroline's cries.

Thomas continued to travel back and forth, working his land when he was not petitioning for the right to post bail for his four older children. His efforts left him with little time to care for young Hannah. But it was a circumstance much preferred when compared to the fate of others.

Many more of Andover's children were locked away with their mothers, and sometimes fathers too. Caroline heard the news of each when Thomas was able to visit, or when she was compelled to seek provisions within Andover's town center. But she did not go into the town center often. Not after the touch test the residents of Andover had conducted. It had been a horrifying spectacle, watching as those who were accused touched the afflicted. If the pains stopped, then it was considered proof enough of the accused's guilt and they were taken away.

But above all else, Caroline missed John. And the guilt of her longing always found her in town as people whispered, "*witch hunter's wife*," behind her back. She was not shunned. But there was a sense of wariness when the others were about her. She feared she would always be known as thus.

Knocking drifted up the stairs into her bedroom. She stifled a groan as she rolled her body onto its side before lifting it out of the momentary comforts of her bed.

"Goody Choate?" An older man spoke, his words muffled through the door. He knocked again. "Goody Choate, are you at home? We wish to speak to you."

Caroline stepped with awkward feet down the stairs. She paused at the door though as more male voices could be heard.

"It is too early to call, Reverend. We should not bother her at this hour."

"We should be on our way if we wish to file this in Salem today."

"She is not likely to help. The Choates are witch hunters. She would never add her signature to it."

Caroline was not dressed in a state for visitors, but her wrapped coat would have to do for the men. She did not wish to hear them discussing her anymore. She opened the door with more determination than she had felt since Bridget's death.

Outside stood a group of bearded surprised faces, and behind them the ragged faces of children and youth. Andover's ministers, Reverend Dane and Reverend Barnard, were at the front, the two of them looking the least surprised at her appearance. Behind them were several other men from the town. The Osgoods. The Chandlers. Goodman Tyler,

Frye, Barker, Davis, and many others. Each one Caroline knew to have a wife or sister awaiting trial in Salem.

"Good morning." Reverend Dane nodded with his greeting. "We are sorry to disturb you so early, Goody Choate. Might we come inside?"

Caroline's gaze did a quick pass over the crowd again. The size of it made her hesitate. "You must keep quiet if you do. Hannah is still sleeping."

"Hannah?"

"Hannah Carrier. Thomas's youngest."

A few of the men's eyebrows rose at this knowledge, but no one spoke. Caroline moved aside and the group filed itself into the kitchen. They stayed silent as promised.

She cradled her belly as she turned to each of them. Several of the men stared. Her body had never allowed her to grow this big with the others. "How can I help you, Reverend Dane?"

Reverend Dane motioned to the children and youth huddled behind the men. "The governor has granted Andover's petitions to release these minors so that they may wait for trial outside the squalor of Salem Town's jail."

Caroline's eyes widened. Thomas had been trying for months for this very thing without any success. "All minors?" Her words cracked with hope.

Reverend Dane nodded. "It has taken some time, but yes. We have agreed, as a town, to cover the fees of those families who cannot afford it. I imagine Thomas will be by later today to retrieve Hannah."

"She will be gratified to hear it when she wakes."

Reverend Dane nodded again, clearly pleased so far with the direction of their conversation. "We know the gratitude Thomas feels for you, Goody Choate, for being so willing to care for his daughter during this time. And so we've come to ask if you would care for a few more souls."

Caroline looked into Reverend Dane's eyes to see if he was in earnest. The old man showed no reservations, only confidence.

"Yes." The word escaped her mouth before she had finished considering it. There were twelve rooms in this house. Many unoccupied bedrooms. And most that would be staying looked to be of a self-sufficient age. She would merely be providing food and shelter.

"We have another thing to ask of you, Goody Choate." Reverend Dane's words whispered of warmth and compassion. "Too many in Andover have been arrested without thought to their well-being or to the state of their health as winter descends upon us. We are filing another petition.

One that concerns all the citizens of Andover, not just its children. They should also be released on bail with a promise that they will return for trial when the court reconvenes in the spring."

"That is good of you, Reverend." She glanced at the other men. "And I am sure there are many others in Andover who will be pleased to hear you are adding your voice to this petition."

Reverend Dane cleared his throat. "It is not just these men who have signed the petition. Reverend Barnard and I have signed it. Several women in Andover have signed it too. Those without any relations to the accused. Even those who served as accusers. We believe it will help sway the governor's decision."

Reverend Barnard unfurled an official paper upon Caroline's table. "We would ask you to sign it too, Goody Choate."

*Thump. Thump.*

Caroline pressed against the baby's movements. "Oh, but I cannot. To care for children is one thing, but John – "

She could not bring herself to finish her sentence as the words warred with her thoughts. John would not wish it.

*Thump. Thump.*

But John was not here. And his obsession with these trials and the notion that they could rid her of her body's curse had brought a new guilt upon Caroline. One she realized now she could possibly relieve herself of with only ink and quill.

All were silent as she stared at the other signatures. Reverend Barnard eased the paper closer to her, its crinkles scraping against the wood of the table as he did so. He set a quill on top.

Her fingers floated above it before she found her grip and brushed the tip into the ink. Then with an unsteady hand she wrote her name.

*Caroline Choate*

Her handwriting stared back at her, a bold declaration. Men shuffled in shame behind her. They had not believed she would do it. A few cleared their throats.

*Thump. Thump. Thump.*

When the men left for Salem, Caroline swept through the twelve rooms of the house, preparing what she could for those who needed a place to stay while their mothers and fathers were held in prison for crimes of witchcraft.

Even with the other children there, Hannah cleaned beside Caroline, contributing where a three-year-old could. Caroline's discomfort had slowly increased these past months as her stomach grew. But today her body ached almost to distraction. There was a tightness in her muscles, and her hips swayed several times whenever she stood still in thought.

The kitchen was stocked and would provide enough food for all who had been brought there. There were pallets in each bedroom with blankets to spare. The main hearth in the house had been swept and provided enough warmth during the autumnal nights, but the others would need to be cleaned out so each room could be occupied this winter.

Caroline bent over one of the hearths now, prepared to wipe the dust of summer away from the stones, when the beginnings of a familiar pain made her whole body clench.

"No." She closed her eyes as tightness grasped around her middle. "No, no." Her middle turned into a solid ball as her pain crested then released.

She was frozen on all fours as she waited for another. Two minutes. Three minutes. Five. She dared not move as she fought against the panic pumping through her veins.

"Goody Choate." Hannah's sweet voice made Caroline flinch. "I'm hungry."

She took a deep breath, trying to clear her mind. "We ate less than an hour ago, Hannah."

"But I'm still hungry."

She took another steadying breath. She knew she shouldn't capitulate to the girl's whims, but it was hard to summon a convincing reminder of why to her panicked mind. "There is a basket of plums in the kitchen. That should be all you need until supper."

"Will you come with me, Goody Choate?"

Caroline shook her head. "You can get it yourself. Or ask one of the other children to go with you."

"Can I eat it in here?"

Caroline had lost count of the minutes since her first pain. "That is fine." The loss of the little control she had from counting left her far too open to her fears. She breathed. She clenched her eyes. The patter of little feet echoed in her mind. Hannah's voice sounded, but Caroline could not hear the words above the warnings her body was screaming.

Hannah's little hand rested on her shoulder, adding a calming weight. Caroline covered it with her own and focused on the sensation of the girl's sticky fingers from the plum juices.

"Goody Choate?" One of the older children spoke, her voice tentative and filled with concern.

Caroline took a final deep breath before opening her eyes. Sweet red juices dripped from Hannah's mouth. She released a shaky smile. "All is well." She stood and addressed the girl. "Is there something you need, Ruth?" She was one of the older ones, nearly sixteen if Caroline had to guess.

"There is a man here. He wishes to speak to you."

Caroline's heart pounded in her chest for a different reason. Anticipation of another sort. Had John come home at last? She made her way to the front door, Ruth and Hannah trailing her determined steps.

But it was not John at the door. It was Thomas Carrier.

Disappointment pooled in Caroline's belly. It had been two months and still John had not come for her.

"Da!" Hannah bounded ahead of Caroline and ran into his arms. Thomas lost himself in the smell of his baby girl before returning for Caroline's greeting.

He turned back to Hannah. "I've come to take you home, love."

Hannah gave a cheer and Caroline smiled at the picture the two of them made. "How are the others?"

"They've eaten their fill and cleaned themselves up. They will rest well tonight in their own beds." Thomas glanced at Ruth before turning to Caroline again. "Is everything well here?"

Her hand instinctively came up to her belly. The pain had yet to come again and she began to doubt its existence. It wouldn't be the first time she had been plagued with such imaginings. “All is well. I have a full house at last.” She looped her arm through Ruth’s.

“Very well.” Thomas lifted Hannah into his arms. “We’re just down the road though, should you need anything.”

Caroline took a steady breath, fighting against tears as Thomas walked away with Hannah. Ruth stayed beside her, allowing Caroline to lead them back inside. The girl had a natural motherly instinct and she thanked Ruth’s upbringing for it. It would be a welcome skill these next few weeks as she attempted to get everyone settled.

As the two of them turned the corner, the tightness grasped around her middle once more. An aching pain accompanied it. She paused, squeezing Ruth’s arm as she breathed through the pain.

“Goody Choate?”

“Yes?”

“Are you well?”

“Yes, Ruth.” Caroline took a deep breath as the tightening released her. “I think I need to lie down though. Can you see to the others? Make sure they are fed and comfortable when night comes? I am sure I overexerted myself and will likely fall asleep once I lie down.”

Ruth nodded, though she insisted on seeing Caroline to her room. She blessed Ruth for her thoughtfulness as she settled into bed. Then she braced herself as the door closed and the tightening pains began again. She vowed she would not cry out and cause any of the children more terror than they had already endured. Still, her fears mounted as inevitability haunted the regular rhythms of her pains.

Her body knew its part. It needed no more than to be locked in the comfort of her own room. But as the sun finished setting, darkness enveloped Caroline with living nightmares and her room became her prison. Visions of blood-stained blankets and too small babies filled her bed. Their gasping breaths echoed in her ears.

"No." She gasped between pains as she fought against her memories. "No, no, no."

She forced her thoughts to Martha. To Bridget. And even to Tituba, whose innocent life still waited behind bars for a sentence. Where had they gone wrong? What manner of evil had persuaded itself into their lives? But Caroline feared she already knew. The Devil had been raised among them – among all who lived in Salem, Andover, and the surrounding villages. He had heard Caroline's name written upon the petition. And now he was here, at her door. She had spoken too little, too late.

"Confess!" The crowd's words carried on the wind. "Confess!"

Lifeless bodies threatened to push at Caroline's entrance. The witches of Salem had come for the witch hunter's wife. She could feel them now, clawing at her body, ripping her from the inside as they demanded more for her sacrifice.

"Stop!" She cried out. "Please, stop!" But her body had been possessed by their specters, tightening with purposes beyond her control until her body broke.

A sudden weight settled in the bed. The beginnings of daylight floated through the window to reveal a baby, silent and pale upon the bloodied quilt. Elijah Choate was born.

## ANDOVER, OCTOBER 18TH, 1692

The world was quiet. Not even the trees quaked. The late autumnal breeze was absent under the beating midday sun. It would be the only silence afforded to Caroline that day.

She tapped the last of the dirt upon its mound, careful not to disturb the bloodied quilt buried beneath. And then she gathered her tools, basket and skirts, and made her way to the house. Her nightmares had not ceased after Elijah's birth. It seemed the curse of the Salem house had followed her to Andover. Her heart hurt at the thought of leaving her children's graves, but she knew she could not stay. Only her promise to care for Andover's children kept her in place.

For the past seven days, Caroline's home had been filled with the footsteps of others. Slowly, the children and youth brought to her had warmed back to life, chattering more of inconsequential things as the air outside grew colder: the color of skirts, baked goods, the addition of animal companions, and contests of strength. A sense of wariness lingered only in their pauses. Each of their trials would be forthcoming in the spring.

Heavy footsteps broke into Caroline's thoughts and she glanced up. She stopped short as John appeared before her at last.

"Caroline."

John's graying beard had lengthened in their months apart. His clothes were well-tailored but modest, as if all were as it should be. But his posture was slightly stooped, giving him an air of intensity. His height allowed him to lean above her.

"Hello, John." Her arms ached to hold him – to be held by him. So much had happened and she'd had no one to unburden herself to. But the anger on his face made Caroline keep such longings to herself. He had not come to make amends.

"You signed the petition."

"I did."

John fought with his words, his fists clenching and unclenching at his sides. His gaze moved over her softened middle, still slightly swollen from her last pregnancy. Then it flickered to the bloodstained basket and tools in her hands. She flinched as he looked beyond her, where the evidence of her work mounded up like the other seven beside it.

"Confess, Caroline." John's words hissed through his teeth. "You have made a great mistake. You shall never keep a child. Those witches will continue to curse you while they are allowed to roam free."

"No, they have given me no curse." She reached out to touch him, but John wrenched his arm away from her reach.

"Do not touch me."

A tear slipped from her eye. Knowing what she must do did not make it hurt any less. "They do not deserve to suffer in their conditions." She took a deep breath. "I wish to use part of the earnings from my cows to purchase the slave, Tituba. Reverend Samuel Parris has refused to pay her bail, but my purchase could give her release."

"You know how I despise the use of slaves."

His jaw worked beneath his beard as they stood in silence. His pride would not allow him reason, so she did not speak. And his heart was blinded by hurt, so she did not console. But John did not stay silent for long.

"After all I have done for you. You have chosen this? You would stand beside them instead of me? Your husband?"

"I would stand with my conscience. But I cannot abide here any longer than I've already promised. Please, John. I wish to leave Salem – to leave Andover. I wish to start over anew."

"I will not leave Salem. I will not abandon what we have built. They cannot chase me away from it. I will have what is rightfully ours here in Andover and in Salem." His eyes dropped daggers into her soul. "If you leave, it will be grounds for desertion. Our marriage will be at its end. Is that what you want?"

"I cannot stay, John. Please listen. I have promised to care for these children, but after – "

"No, Caroline. If this is your wish, to care for accused witches and to abandon all we have built here, then I –" He swallowed his words before beginning again. "I want nothing to do with you."

His eyes found hers and her heart broke anew at the pain she saw there. But he did not hold her gaze for long. His attention moved to the twelve-room house beside them.

"You may stay here through winter." John's voice was softer now. Distant. Civil. A whisper of a mask for his hurt. "I will not return to work the land until next spring, after the trials have ended. I am not so heartless as to leave you with nothing."

Caroline nodded, and she braced herself for the words she knew he would speak next.

"Goodbye, Caroline."

John left, untying his horse from a tree before riding south. She released her guilt as he faded from her sight for the final time. When she turned to the house, Ruth stood in the doorway, a newborn baby bundled with fresh linens crying in her arms.

## Afterword

In the years of 1692 and 1693, an estimated, and unprecedented, 200 people were accused of witchcraft within the Massachusetts Bay Colony. Over 140 of them stood for trial in Salem Town. Most confessed their guilt while being questioned under duress. Thirty of the individuals who insisted upon their innocence were declared guilty and twenty five of them died as a result of the trials.

It is a harrowing event in history that has persisted throughout the centuries, capturing our curiosity and producing many theories, stories, and reproductions. I, like many others, have always been fascinated by the Salem Witch Trials. But this story didn't start until after a discussion I had with a couple of friends where I learned both of them were direct descendants of some of the accused.

It is a common thing for the descendants of these people to visit the sites in Salem Massachusetts but I began to wonder, what about the descendants of those who had made the accusations? From there my mind spiraled into several compounding what ifs. The question as I have always known it was, what if you were accused of witchcraft? Or, what if your neighbor/

friend/brother/sister were accused?

But what if, instead, you were the one placing blame? Or perhaps, what if someone you loved was offering their testimony against the "witches" of Salem? What would you do? I'd like to think that I would have said something against the unfair accusations. But life has taught me that you can't truly know what your actions would/will be until you are faced with a similar situation. I knew my family had ties to the area around the same time period as the trials, and as I pondered these questions I had the distinct suspicion that my family may have been on the wrong side of history. And I was right.

Samuel Martin of Andover is my 11th great-grandfather. He was one of the principal accusers of Mary Ayer Parker, who was hanged for witchcraft on September 22nd, 1692. I have no records outlining what motivations he had for such an accusation. Nor do I have records surrounding his reason for later signing the same petition Caroline signed in support of the accused. I can only speculate his thoughts and feelings on the matter. This petition though, and the ones that followed, became a swift and solid foundation in the defense of the accused. It stopped the hysteria from spreading further in the Massachusetts Bay Colony and it brought the trials to the attention of many prominent figures – including Samuel Willard, Thomas Brattle, and Governor William Phips – who ultimately brought the trials to a close.

The image of Caroline lying in bed pregnant while others were being hung outside came from a real situation I found when combing through the genealogical records of the people in the Massachusetts Bay Colony. A man named John Symonds was born in 1692 in Salem Massachusetts. He claimed that his mother, Sarah, was able to see Gallows Hill outside her bedroom window as she laid resting in bed with him.

Outside of the Choate family, all characters named in this story were real people. These events did happen to them and the words from several of their trials can be found in the transcripts made available online for free by the University of Virginia in their *Salem Witch Trials Documentary Archive and Transcription Project* if you wish to check them and other resources out for yourself. A copy of the transcripts can also be purchased online through Amazon.

Even for a short project such as this, a great deal of research had to be done. Resources outside of the ones mentioned above include Richard Hite's book, *In the Shadow of Salem*, Elaine G. Breslaw's book, *Tituba, Reluctant Witch of Salem*, the collection of essays, *The Intellectual Culture of Puritan Women, 1558-1680*, the many lectures by historian Margo Burns, The Salem Witch Museum in Salem Massachusetts, The History of Massachusetts Blog (History of Massachusetts Blog), walking tours of the area available on YouTube, and many other various sources. Any mistakes or misinterpretations within this book are entirely of my own and should not reflect on the quality of the resources listed above.

As is always the case, I have several individuals to thank. Fellow authors Amanda Fetters, K.B. MacNeille, Liz Davis, Sheila Bliss, Stephanie Koathes, my editor Julia Allen, and my family members all helped with corrections, suggestions, and encouragement. Without their efforts, and the efforts of many others, this story certainly wouldn't be where it is today.

If you would like to take the discussion further, check out the suggested questions on my website at Reader Guides – Jessica Lunt | The Official Site of Author Jessica Lunt (jessicalunt.com/readerguides)

## About the Author

Jessica Lunt grew up in Arizona, but since becoming a military spouse, has enjoyed living the nomadic lifestyle. When not writing, she takes advantage of exploring whatever part of the world she's in by napping with cheetahs, racing through the DMZ, and singing the U.S. national anthem in front of the original Star-Spangled Banner, among many other things. But her four young children weren't truly impressed with her until she wrote a book.

**Stay connected**
**Mailing List:** Newsletter – Jessica Lunt | The Official Site of Author Jessica Lunt
**Goodreads:** Jessica Lunt (Author of The Witch Hunter's Wife) | Goodreads
**Facebook:** Facebook
**Instagram:** https://www.instagram.com/jlunt2
**Threads:** Jessica Lunt (@jlunt2) • Threads, Say more
**Email:** authorjessicalunt@gmail.com

www.ingramcontent.com/pod-product-compliance
Lightning Source LLC
Chambersburg PA
CBHW030602310726
48979CB00003B/538

* 9 7 8 1 9 6 9 1 9 5 0 0 6 *